"I RAISED MY HAND!"

Starting First Grade

Tracey Klehr

To order additional copies of this book, contact:
Xlibris Corporation
1-888-795-4274
www.Xlibris.com
Orders@Xlibris.com

DEDICATION

To my husband Chuck, whose endless,
true love has made my life wonderful and complete.
To my children Emelie, Danielle and Charles,
for being the best part of my life.
To my Mom, for being my best friend; your love,
support and laughter we share is not replaceable.
And to the following children and teachers that
will always be in my heart.

Emilie	Jesse
Chariotte	James
Daniel	Grace
Olivia	Jack
Josephine	Noah
Ana	Caroline
Dylan	Jessica
Madeleine	Avielle
Catherine	Benjamin
Chase	Allison

Rachel Davino, Dawn Hochsprung, Anne Marie Murphy,
Lauren Rousseau, Mary Sheriach and Victoria Soto

"Emma!" her Mom called, "come outside and see what I have found!" Emma jumped from the kitchen chair startling her dog from its nap. She slid the screen door open, quickly made her way across the patio and into the backyard. There was a cool breeze and the clear blue sky allowed the sun to sparkle off the trees. With her dog way ahead of her, Emma joined her Mom under the big Maple tree.

Emma's eyes followed her Mom's finger, which pointed to the ground. In the dark green grass Emma saw a little hump of brown and gold. As the crickets chirped in the backyard her Mom said, "It's a box turtle!"

Emma squatted down as low as her knees would allow and got as close to the turtle as she could. " Where is its head?" she asked her Mom, "Is it hiding?" "Yes, I think so," said her mom, "unless it's taking a nap," she added. Emma looked over at her dog, who now sleeps most of the day.

"Can we pick it up?" Emma asked. "Yes!" her Mom replied, "but we have to be very careful." Her Mom put her fingers on either side of the turtle's shell and slowly lifed it from the grass. Emma heard a *Hiss* sound as the front of the turtle's shell shut tight.

"Why is it so shy?" Emma asked. "Because we are something new to the turtle, it may have never been picked up by a person before," said her Mom. "Can we keep it?" Emma wondered. "Well, I don't think the turtle would like that," her Mom continued, "we should just let it go on its way so it can grow up the way turtles like to."

Emma agreed and added, "It would not be able to have as much fun and meet other turtles." Emma realized that the turtle could only learn new things and grow strong by exploring new places. The turtle would not be able to do that in a box or small garden.

As Emma wished the turtle good luck her Mom said, "We need to go to the grocery store. You start first grade tomorrow and I would like you to pick out some healthy food for breakfast and for your lunch box." As they walked up the patio steps towards the kitchen door her Mom added, "You are going to be at school all day, so eating healthy will be important."

Emma lowered her head into her shoulders. Just the thought of being in school all day and away from her home made her nervous. "You look like the turtle," her Mom said, "why do you feel like you have to go into your shell?" Emma looked up at her Mom and said, "I won't be home, I won't have you, and I don't know what's going to happen each day," said Emma.

"Well, think of it this way," her Mom replied. "When we put that turtle back down into the grass and said 'good luck,' the turtle is now going to explore, make new friends, and have a great day. That is what you get to do at school, but you will have a lunch box and a back pack," her Mom added, "besides, you will be able to tell me and your Daddy all about it when you get home."

Emma lowered her shoulders and raised her head as she realized her Mom was right. "But I am still a little nervous," she said. "Of course," said her Mom in a soft voice, "but starting first grade is exciting too."

As Emma and her Mom entered the grocery store, the first thing they saw were all of the colorful fruits and vegetables. "This is a good place to start," her Mom said. Emma walked over and held up a bumpy, green thing. "What is this Mommy?" she asked curiously.

"That is an Avocado," her Mom announced. "You can eat this?" Emma questioned. "Yes, would you like to try one?" "Sure," Emma replied, putting it into their shopping cart as she walked towards the apples and oranges. Not only did they choose some great food, her Mom let her pick out a new box of crayons and color pencils.

Later on at the dinner table, Emma's Daddy asked her if she was ready for first grade. "Tomorrow should be a nice day...a nice day for school that is. Are you ready?" Emma replied with her shoulders up by her ears, "Well I'm excited, but a little nervous too." As her Daddy brought his empty plate over to the sink he said, "Everyone is a little nervous." Giving Emma a kiss on the top of her head as he passed by he added, "Just think of what you are excited about."

Emma's Mom had a great idea. "We can make a list of all the things you are excited about for first grade," she explained. After clearing the dinner table, Emma was happy to start her list. She wrote: 1. **Make a friend** 2. **Go on playground** 3. ***** **Raise my hand**. Emma put a star next to the last one.

That night Emma and her Mom picked out what she would wear on her first day of school. A new purple shirt with a new pair of shorts were perfect. It was going to be warm by the afternoon, so she put out her favorite pair of sandals.

After reading a book with her Mom and Dad, Emma gave her dog a hug and got right into bed. As she started to fall asleep, Emma suddenly jumped out of bed and switched her sandals for sneakers. "Just in case I need to run fast on the playground," Emma said to her stuffed elephant.

"Emma, time to rise and shine for school!" her Mom said as she entered her bedroom. She could hear her dog's tail wagging against the door frame. Emma sprang out of bed and was ready for school in no time!

Holding onto the side rail while lifting her foot up onto the first step of the bus, Emma was glad she wore sneakers. She was able to sit right next to the window and wave back to her Mom.

Emma had driven down this road a hundred times, but this trip was different. As the wheels of the bus rolled over the bumps in the road, Emma felt her legs lift off her seat. Sitting so high above the ground she could see the squirrels running from tree branch to tree branch. The other children's voices faded over the roar of the engine as the bus reached the top of the hill.

When the bus came to a slow stop, Emma felt important knowing that the cars had to obey the bus's signal to stop too. The door opened and a few more children climbed aboard. The children's eyes were wide and their smiles would come and go as they, like Emma, were also excited and a little nervous.

When Emma walked into her classroom the teacher was waiting to greet her. Emma's name was printed in colorful, bold letters on her desk. As she sat down, the girl sitting next to her said, "Hi, my name is Annabel, I like your backpack." Emma smiled and said, "I'm Emma, I like your backpack too."

"Good morning boys and girls, welcome to first grade!" said Emma's teacher with a big smile. "I would like to start our day with you getting to know your classmates," the teacher continued, "getting to know each other will make you feel more comfortable and you may make a friend along the way. Lets start with your neighbor. I would like each of you to ask your neighbor two questions that you would like to know about one another," Emma's teacher explained.

Emma began by asking her neighbor Annabel, "Do you have a pet?" Annabel said, "Yep, I have a cat named Freckles." Emma's second question was: What do you like to do for fun? Annabel shyly answered, "I like to read books and play outside." Emma announced, "Me too!" Then Annabel asked Emma the same questions. Emma answered, "I have fun playing with my dog Haley, and I like to do arts and crafts."

Emma and Annabel looked at their teacher with big smiles as they both felt like they had just made a new friend. Then the teacher said, "Now boys and girls I would like you to spend some time meeting your other classmates." Emma not only met Annabel, but also made friends with Danielle and Charles!

Before Emma knew it, it was lunch time and then onto the playground! It felt good to be outside in the fresh air. At first Emma stood quietly looking around, she was not sure what to do. There was so much to choose from and everyone was running in different directions. But then some of her new friends waved her over to the swing set.

Emma loved the swings! Pumping her legs back and forth; she felt like she was flying through the air!

Next, Emma and her friends ran over to the jungle gym. Holding on tight with each step she climbed higher and higher. Emma liked being half way up and thought she would save going to the top for another day. Emma's teacher blew her whistle and asked for her class to line up at the door to go inside. Emma was excited to go back to her classroom and was curious to see what her teacher had planned.

As the class settled down in their seats, the teacher started to talk about all the fun things that they are going to learn this year. "Boys and girls, let's begin today with learning how to write some new words. This year we will learn to spell and use words that start with each letter of the alphabet."

"We will begin with the letter A," the teacher continued. "I am going to write words on the board that start with the letter *A* that you used *all* the time when writing." *All* was put on the board. *Also, Away,* and *About* were soon added to the list.

"Now, I would like you to think of a word that starts with the letter *A*, that you do not use every day," said Emma's teacher. The classroom was silent. All of her classmates looked around the room for ideas. Emma's eyes got real big as she thought of a word. She knew it was a great word and it would be a perfect answer!

Emma's head went down into her shoulders as she looked at her teacher. "Anyone?" the teacher asked. Emma knew this was it. Taking one last look around the room, she slowly stretched her arm way above her head. The teacher looked at her and said, "Yes Emma, do you have a word?" Emma felt her shoulders drop, and with her head held high she answered her teacher excitedly "...Avocado!" "Wow, what a great word!" said her teacher with a big smile.

Emma stepped down from her school bus and headed across her front lawn. As her Mom headed towards her, Emma laughed as her dog sprang up and down with excitement. With a big hug Emma and her Mom said to each other, "I missed you."

As Emma's dog was wiggling on its back in the fresh cut grass, her Mom eagerly asked, "How was your first day of first grade?" Emma was so excited to tell her Mom and Dad all about her day.

As Emma walked up her front porch steps, she suddenly stopped and said, "Guess what?...I RAISED MY HAND!"

CPSIA information can be obtained
at www.ICGtesting.com
Printed in the USA
LVIC06n0217050814
397572LV00003B/3